Disney · PIXAR

TOY STORY

Woody's

Augmented Reality ADVENTURE

CARLTON KiDS

HOW TO USE THIS BOOK

Are you ready to enter a top-secret world where **toys come to life?**

Simply download the FREE app *TOY STORY BOOK WITH AR.* **Then open it on your mobile device.**

Scan every page to find your *Toy Story* friends and other surprises!

Meet Woody, Buzz, Bo Peep, the Aliens and more in 3D!

Scan this page in the app to get started!

WOODY

Howdy partner! Andy's favourite toy is Sheriff Woody Pride, a brave and kind cowboy. He was once the star of a rootin' tootin' TV show, saving the day with his loyal gang. Now he lives in Andy's house and is the leader of the toys. He is really smart, but can also be a little bossy!

COWBOY HAT

BANDANA

CHECKED SHIRT

SHERIFF'S BADGE

WAISTCOAT

COWBOY CATCHPHRASES

There's a pull-string voice box on Woody's back. Here are some of the things he might say if you pull his string:

"SOMEBODY'S POISONED THE WATERHOLE!"

"THERE'S A SNAKE IN MY BOOT!"

"You're my favourite deputy!"

"This town ain't big enough for the two of us!"

WILD WEST WARDROBE

Woody always wears his Sheriff's uniform – though sometimes he loses his hat!

BOOTS AND SPURS

DENIM TROUSERS

Woody, Jessie and Bullseye were all in the old TV show Woody's Roundup!

A SPEEDY STEED

Neigh! Bullseye was Woody's trusty horse back in the Roundup days. He has stayed loyal to his cowboy friend over the years and would still follow him anywhere. Bullseye is always full of energy and bounds around Andy's bedroom like a playful puppy.

PICK UP WOODY!

VIEW THESE PAGES THROUGH THE APP ON YOUR PHONE OR TABLET, AND WOODY WILL APPEAR, READY TO PLAY!

JESSIE

Cowgirl Jessie is loud, loyal and she just loves to have fun. When faced with a tricky situation, Jessie can be relied upon to come up with a rootin' tootin' solution. Although she's pretty fearless, one thing that does scare her is small spaces. She was kept in a box in storage for so long that she now has claustrophobia.

Yodel-ay-ee-oooo!

DARING DOLL

Yee-haw! Another member of Woody's *Roundup* gang, Jessie is a pull-string cowgirl. Woody is like her brother and she is really good pals with his horse, Bullseye. Jessie is full of energy and loves to go on daring adventures. When she is happy or excited, she yodels!

ROOTIN' TOOTIN' ROMANCE

When Buzz Lightyear met Jessie, he fell for her good looks and adventurous personality. When Buzz got switched to Spanish mode, he danced his way into Jessie's heart too!

RIGHT-HAND GAL

Whenever Woody finds himself in a spot of bother, he can count on cowgirl Jessie to give him a helping hand. Never afraid to take charge, Jessie can be a bit of a bossy boots but she has a big heart. She is brave and brainy, always able to think her way out of trouble and save her toy pals.

HORSE HUGS

Although he is and always will be Woody's horse, Bullseye is also really close to cowgirl Jessie. They spend a lot of time together and she is the one he turns to for a comforting hug – or to hide behind! – when he's feeling scared.

Jessie and Bullseye

SCAN ALL THE PAGES WITH WOODY'S BADGE TO HELP HIM UNLOCK A SECRET NEW CHARACTER!

BUZZ

Space ranger Buzz landed in Andy's life on the little boy's 7th birthday. An awesome astronaut action figure, he used to be the lead character in Buzz Lightyear of Star Command, a space-themed TV show. The other toys look up to Buzz and think the intergalactic explorer is super cool. His favourite saying is,

"To infinity and beyond!"

GLOW IN THE DARK SPACE SUIT

SPACE RANGER LIGHTYEAR

BLAST BUZZ'S LASER!
VIEW THESE PAGES THROUGH THE APP ON YOUR PHONE OR TABLET TO SEE BUZZ AND PRESS HIS BUTTONS!

HELPFUL HERO

As a space ranger, Buzz is sworn to protect the galaxy from the Evil Emperor Zurg and all other threats. He takes his role super seriously and will always do his very best to help a toy in trouble.

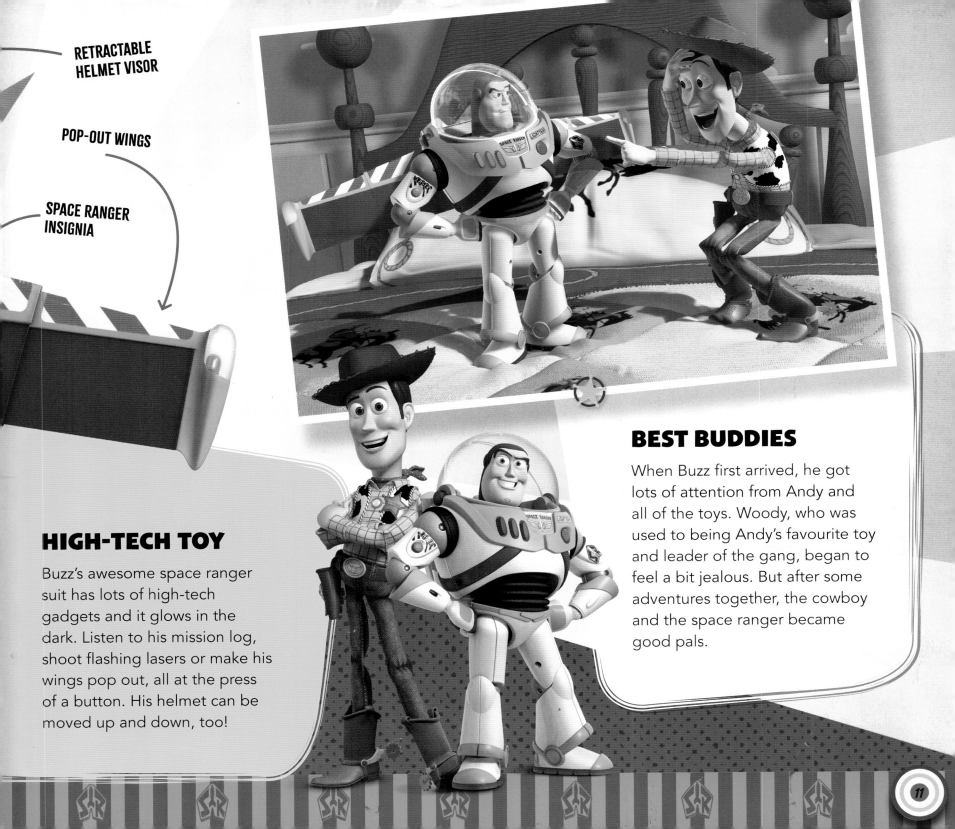

RETRACTABLE
HELMET VISOR

POP-OUT WINGS

SPACE RANGER
INSIGNIA

HIGH-TECH TOY

Buzz's awesome space ranger
suit has lots of high-tech
gadgets and it glows in the
dark. Listen to his mission log,
shoot flashing lasers or make his
wings pop out, all at the press
of a button. His helmet can be
moved up and down, too!

BEST BUDDIES

When Buzz first arrived, he got
lots of attention from Andy and
all of the toys. Woody, who was
used to being Andy's favourite toy
and leader of the gang, began to
feel a bit jealous. But after some
adventures together, the cowboy
and the space ranger became
good pals.

BARBIE *and* KEN

Plastic fantastic! With their collection of cool clothes, lovebirds Barbie and Ken are the most fashionable dolls in the toy box. Although it was love at first sight, their romance has had some rocky patches – Barbie didn't like it when Ken was hanging around with a bad crowd, but luckily she realised he's a good guy really.

DUO'S DREAMHOUSE

Ken has lived in the Dream House for a long time and when Barbie moves in, he's so happy to finally have someone to share it with. With a disco and a dune buggy, plus a whole room just for trying on clothes, it has everything a doll could want!

PLASTIC PAIR

Bubbly Barbie is always full of energy and she wears brightly-coloured fitness clothes with stripy leg warmers – plus hot pink high heels!

LOVE WINS

She might look sweet and soft, but Barbie's no pushover! Barbie broke up with Ken when she discovered he was part of Lotso's gang, a bunch of mean bullies. When Ken took her side, the two became boyfriend and girlfriend again. Together they took over as the new leaders of Sunnyside and made it a nice play for toys to live.

The Green ARMY MEN

The Green Army Men might only have one outfit – their uniform – but looking good is the last thing on their minds. They are small in size, but they're big on bravery. These fearless little guys live to protect their toy pals.

BUCKET O' SOLDIERS

In a bucket in Andy's bedroom, 200 little soldiers lived. Led by Sarge, they were made of hard green plastic and had a board between their feet. But being stuck in set positions didn't slow the Green Army Men down! They were often sent out on missions and reported back, using baby monitors to talk to the other toys.

OVER AND OUT

When they realized Andy has grown up and they wouldn't be played with anymore, the Green Army Men who hadn't been lost or thrown away over the years decided to parachute out the window. Sarge and two paratroopers eventually landed in the playground at Sunnyside Daycare, where they met Barbie and Ken.

A GOOD SOLDIER NEVER LEAVES A MAN BEHIND.

REX

Unlike a real Tyrannosaurus, scaredy-dinosaur toy Rex is gentle, kind and caring and he hates any arguments or confrontations. Always nervous, Rex worries about *everything*, especially his small roar.

TIMID T-REX

He might be made of hard and heavy plastic, but Rex is really a big softy. With his teeny tiny roar, he's all teeth and no bite. Rex worries that he's not scary enough and will be replaced by a more ferocious dinosaur toy...

GRRR-EAT GAMERS

Rex enjoys playing computer games and he's pretty good. When he moved to Bonnie's house, he became best pals with her toy dinosaur, Trixie. She shares his love of gaming and the pair spend lots of time playing together.

HAMM

Confident piggy bank Hamm is never afraid to tell the other toys exactly what he thinks of them. He is a wisecracking joker with a wicked and slightly sarcastic sense of humour.

FUNNY PIGGY

Hamm is a pink plastic piggy bank, with a cork that keeps coins inside his belly. Ever the entertainer, Hamm plays tunes on the harmonica and tells the toys loads of jokes. He especially enjoys making fun of his friend Rex over his endless fears and worries.

EVIL GENIUS

Wearing a little black hat – borrowed from Mr Potato Head – Hamm often had a starring role in Andy's adventures. Although he had fun playing the bad guy known as Evil Dr. Porkchop, Hamm always tells the toys that crime doesn't pay.

FILL HAMM WITH COINS!

VIEW THESE PAGES THROUGH THE APP ON YOUR PHONE OR TABLET, AND HAMM WILL APPEAR RIGHT ON YOUR BOOK!

SLINKY DOG

As well as his horse, Bullseye, Woody has a puppy pal. With his strong and stretchy body, Slinky Dog has some cool skills and abilities that always come in handy on the toys' many adventures. He's a totally woof-tastic toy!

PLAYFUL PUP

Toy sausage dog Slinky is a wooden sausage dog with floppy ears, a green collar and a stretchy coil of metal in his middle. He's as energetic and playful as a real pup, and faithful like one too. One of his favourite pastimes is playing a board game called checkers with his cowboy pal, Woody.

GADDILY BOB-HOWDY!

PAWSOME TRICKS

Between Slinky's head and his bottom is a stretchy coil body made of metal. It's super strong and so the other toys can use him like a bungee cord, jumping down and then bouncing back up. Sometimes Slinky also uses his flexible middle section to tie up toys when they're behaving badly.

WHEEZY

Wheezy the squeezy penguin is a very nervous toy, always worrying about anything and everything. But he is brave enough to sing and he loves to serenade other toys. Andy's bedroom was often filled with the sound of his deep, rich voice.

PUFFED-OUT PENGUIN

Wheezy is made of rubber and wears a smart red bowtie. He was a wonderful singer – until Andy squeezed him too tightly and his squeaker broke. Wheezy was left on a dusty bookshelf, where all the asthmatic penguin could do was cough.

FINDING FRIENDS

One day, Woody's arm was accidentally torn and he was also placed up on the bookshelf. The two old pals were so happy to see each other! When Wheezy was put in a yard sale, Woody came to his rescue. Eventually Wheezy was fixed by a toy called Mr Shark, and so he was able entertain his friends again.

The ALIENS

The Three alien squeeze toys originally came from a claw vending machine in a Pizza Planet restaurant and then became car decorations. When the aliens fell out of a car window, they were saved by Mr Potato Head and went to live with him in Andy's bedroom.

THE CLAW

Andy's three alien toys once lived inside a claw vending machine at Pizza Planet – a close look reveals the restaurant's logo on their blue space uniforms. When Woody and the toys got into big trouble, the aliens spotted 'The Claw' and used it to scoop up their friends, saving the day.

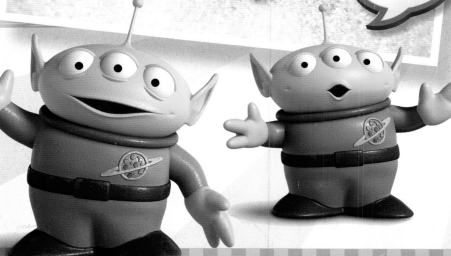

SQUEEZE 'N' SQUEAK

The aliens are made of bouncy green rubber and they make a squeaking sound when squeezed. There are three of them, each with three eyes and three fingers per hand – plus an antenna on top of their head!

STACK UP THE ALIENS!

VIEW THESE PAGES THROUGH THE APP ON YOUR PHONE OR TABLET, AND YOU CAN PICK UP, STACK AND KNOCK OVER THE ALIENS!

Oooh!

Mr and Mrs POTATO HEAD

Even though Mr Potato Head was Andy's toy and Mrs Potato Head was Molly's, they fell madly in love. After Mr Potato Head saved the lives of the three alien squeeze toys, Mrs Potato Head decided to adopt them and they became one happy family!

POTATO PARTS

Mr and Mrs Potato Head have lots of plastic parts that can be mixed up and moved around to make some very funny faces.

It's so nice to have a big, strong spud around the house.

Did you all take stupid pills this morning?

HUMPTY DUMPTY WAS PUSHED!

Son of a building block!

DON'T TALK TO ANY TOY YOU DON'T KNOW!

Alright fellas, let's roll!

NAUGHTY TOYS

During their adventures, Andy's toys sometimes ran into bad guys. These toys could be mean and scary, but Woody and the gang learned that if they worked together then they would be able to escape from evil and get back home.

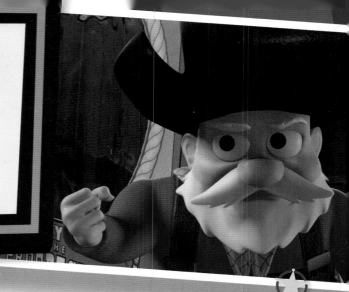

GOLD-DIGGING BAD GUY

Woody, Jessie and Bullseye appeared in the *Roundup* TV show alongside Stinky Pete the Prospector. He is made of plastic and carries a pickaxe, but what makes him extra-special is that he's still in his box and has never been opened. Mint! Smart and sneaky, Stinky Pete tried to stop Woody from getting home.

INTERGALACTIC BAD GUY

Emperor Zurg is an action figure, and Buzz Lightyear's evil archenemy from the *Star Command* TV show. He wears plastic purple robes, a cape, a mask with horns and his eyes glow red. Buzz believed that Zurg was building a secret weapon with enough power to destroy an entire planet, and swore to stop him. But Zurg lived in a fortress and kept track of Buzz's every move…

SWEET-SMELLING BAD GUY

Lots-o'-Huggin' Bear is a large, pink teddy bear that smells of strawberries. At first Lotso seems really fun and friendly, but it's fake. He took over Sunnyside Daycare and ran it with an iron paw, along with his gang of thug toys.

LOTSO'S GANG

To be a member of Lotso's gang, toys had to be super-tough and super-mean!

Sparks

With his flashing red eyes, pincers and rubber wheels, this robot can be really scary. Watch out – he spits out red glowing sparks when he rolls along!

Stretch

A glittery purple octopus must be as pretty on the inside as she is on the outside, right? Wrong. Don't be suckered in by this super-stretchy villainess.

Big Baby

With his big blue eyes and squidgy body, this baby doll looks like a big softy. But really, he's as hard-hearted as the plastic of his head, arms and legs.

Chunk

This orange plastic rock creature has sharp spikes along his shoulders. In the press of a button, his spinning face can change from smile to a snarl.

Twitch

This action figure might look like half insect, half man, but he is *all* evil. With his big muscles, powerful wings and magical battle staff, he's one bad bug.

BO PEEP

Bo Peep may seem sweet natured but don't be fooled – she's no push over! In fact, this delicate porcelain doll is one strong, smart toy with an unbreakable spirit. Bo and her three sheep lived on the base of a reading lamp, until their home was given away.

SEE BO PEEP IN 3D!
VIEW THESE PAGES THROUGH THE APP ON YOUR PHONE OR TABLET, AND BO PEEP WILL APPEAR RIGHT ON YOUR BOOK!

PEEP'S PALS

Bo Peep is a tough-talking shepherdess made of porcelain. She has three mischief-making sheep, called Billy, Goat and Gruff, who are joined together. Bo and her flock actually belonged to Andy's sister, Molly, but they liked to hang out with the other toys. Andy's adventures often had Bo getting into trouble, with hero Woody riding to rescue her.

BILLY

GOAT

GRUFF

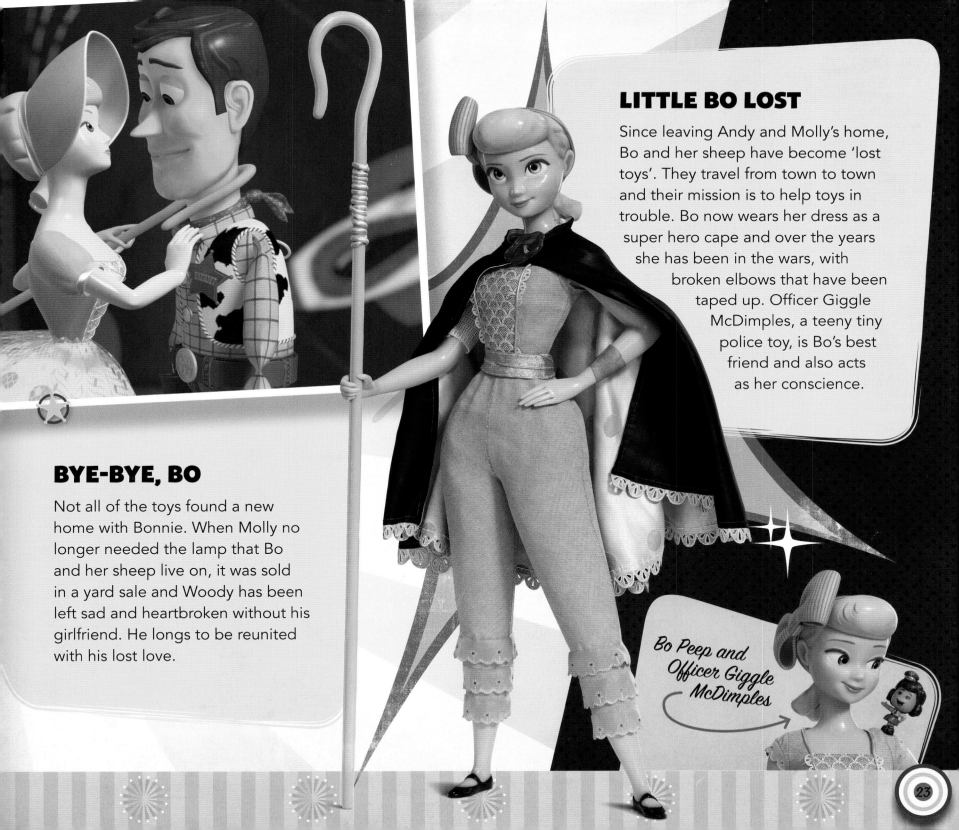

LITTLE BO LOST

Since leaving Andy and Molly's home, Bo and her sheep have become 'lost toys'. They travel from town to town and their mission is to help toys in trouble. Bo now wears her dress as a super hero cape and over the years she has been in the wars, with broken elbows that have been taped up. Officer Giggle McDimples, a teeny tiny police toy, is Bo's best friend and also acts as her conscience.

BYE-BYE, BO

Not all of the toys found a new home with Bonnie. When Molly no longer needed the lamp that Bo and her sheep live on, it was sold in a yard sale and Woody has been left sad and heartbroken without his girlfriend. He longs to be reunited with his lost love.

Bo Peep and Officer Giggle McDimples

23

GABBY GABBY
and the DUMMIES

Back in the 1950s, a talking doll was the must-have toy of the time. Her name is Gabby Gabby and her face was seen on adverts *everywhere.* Since then, she has been stuck inside a display case in an antique store with no toy to talk to!

LOST VOICE

Gabby Gabby has never been owned by a child because even though she looks oh-so sweet, her voice box is broken. Instead, she has lived inside an antique store, feeling lonely and unloved. Gabby Gabby would do anything to find her voice and finally have a happy home.

IT'S A STEAL

When Woody and some pals arrive at the antique store, Gabby Gabby spots his pull-string and has an idea… Gabby Gabby's group of henchmen, some ventriloquist's dummies, are happy to help her steal Woody's voice box, even if it means taking another toy hostage!

OFFICER GIGGLE McDIMPLES

This dinky action figure is a real force for good. Officer Giggle McDimples is chatty, funny and she always tries to do the best thing!

NO DUMMY

Although these ventriloquist's dummies don't do much talking, their actions speak louder than words. With their smart suits, the dummies look like gentlemen, but they don't act like it. They'll do anything for their boss Gabby Gabby!

GOODY GIGGLE

Officer Giggle McDimples might be small, but she has a really huge heart. She is BFFs with Bo Peep and gives her shepherdess pal some very good advice. Spirited, kind and full of fun, Giggle is a talented police officer who works for the Pet Patrol division and wears a blue uniform.

DUKE CABOOM

Vroooom! **Action doll Duke Caboom zooms here and zooms there. A Canadian stunt rider for the 1970s, he has an amazing handlebar moustache and seems to be full of confidence and swagger.**

MAKE DUKE DO CRAZY STUNTS!
VIEW THESE PAGES THROUGH THE APP ON YOUR PHONE OR TABLET, AND YOU CAN MAKE DUKE DO HAIR-RAISING BIKE TRICKS!

DAREDEVIL DUKE

Duke Caboom rides a super cool stunt motorcycle and is a totally fearless daredevil, always doing tricks and jumps on his bike. But not everyone thinks he's the best – he is still sad about being rejected by his kid owner because the advert was better than the reality.

RIDE TO THE RESCUE

When Woody and his pals need help to rescue a toy that's been kidnapped, they turn to Duke Caboom. His mad motorcycle skills will come in handy and the stunt rider is sure to save the day.

DUCKY and BUNNY

Best pals Ducky and Bunny are inseparable – literally!
They're attached to one another by a wing and a paw.
Once a prize at a carnival, the fluffy, furry friends have
been hanging out together for many years.

FUNNY FRIENDS

They've not had the easiest
of rides, so Ducky and Bunny
use jokes to cheer themselves
up. They have a sharp sense of
humour and can find the funny
side of almost any situation.

TOGETHER FOREVER

Although Ducky and Bunny have been
moved from location to location over the
years, there's one thing for sure – they'll
always be together. Not only because
they're physically attached, but because
they're able to keep each other's spirits
up whenever times get tough.

FORKY

This brand new toy is stuck together from all kinds of bits and bobs at Bonnie's kindergarten. He's going to need a lot of help from Woody and his friends to pull himself together!

HOMEMADE HERO

Say hello to the newest toy in town! Forky is made of a spork, a pipe-cleaner, some modelling clay, a couple of googly eyes, and two ice lolly sticks. The only problem is, he's not sure if he's a real toy at all! Forky has a ton of questions about himself and the world around him.

I'm just a fork... or am I?

I'm homemade.

What does it all mean?

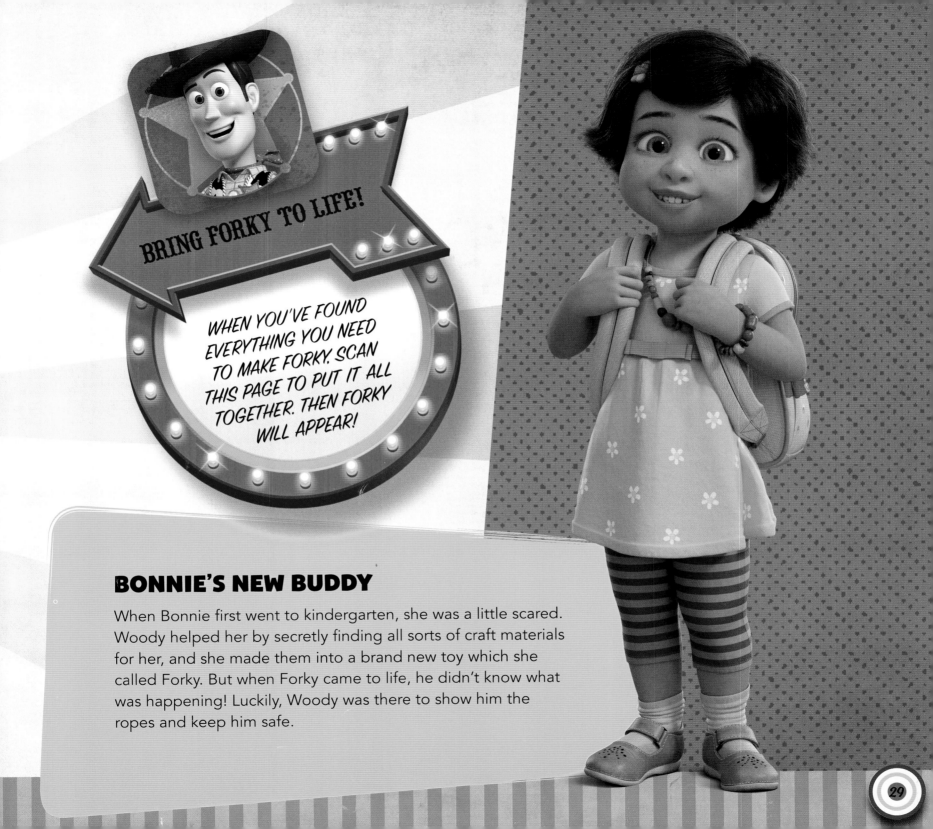

BRING FORKY TO LIFE!

WHEN YOU'VE FOUND EVERYTHING YOU NEED TO MAKE FORKY, SCAN THIS PAGE TO PUT IT ALL TOGETHER. THEN FORKY WILL APPEAR!

BONNIE'S NEW BUDDY

When Bonnie first went to kindergarten, she was a little scared. Woody helped her by secretly finding all sorts of craft materials for her, and she made them into a brand new toy which she called Forky. But when Forky came to life, he didn't know what was happening! Luckily, Woody was there to show him the ropes and keep him safe.

WOODY
and the Gang

By the end of their first adventure together, Woody has introduced Forky to lots of his old friends... and they've made some brand new ones too!